A FIREFLY BOOK

Published by Firefly Books Ltd. 2018

Adapted from the animated short film *Threads* © 2017 Mikrofilm AS and National Film Board of Canada

First Printing

Library of Congress Control Number: 2018932023

Library and Archives Canada Cataloguing in Publication
Kove, Torill, author, illustrator
     Threads / by Torill Kove.
(National Film Board of Canada collection)
Adapted from the film Threads.
ISBN 978-0-228-10081-2 (hardcover)
     I. Title. II. Title: Threads (Motion picture)
PS8621.O9735T47 2018   jC813'.6   C2018-900587-4

Published in Canada by
Firefly Books Ltd.
50 Staples Avenue, Unit 1
Richmond Hill, Ontario L4B 0A7

Published in the United States by
Firefly Books (U.S.) Inc.
P.O. Box 1338, Ellicott Station
Buffalo, New York, USA 14205

The NFB is Canada's public producer of award-winning creative documentaries, auteur animation, interactive stories and participatory experiences. NFB producers are embedded in communities across the country, from St. John's to Vancouver, working with talented creators on innovative and socially relevant projects. The NFB is a leader in gender equity in film and digital media production, and is working to strengthen Indigenous-led production, guided by the recommendations of Canada's Truth and Reconciliation Commission. NFB productions have won over 7,000 awards, including 18 Canadian Screen Awards, 17 Webbys, 12 Oscars and more than 100 Genies. To access NFB works, visit NFB.ca or download our apps for mobile devices

Illustrations by Torill Kove
Interior design by Elisabeth Vold Bjone
Cover design by Noor Majeed
Printed and bound in China

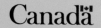 *We acknowledge the financial support of the Government of Canada.*

TORILL KOVE

THREADS

FIREFLY BOOKS

We are all reaching for threads,

threads to connect us with others, threads to
help us find purpose, threads to discover love.

I'm reaching for threads too, and when I see one that looks special, I leap for it.

As it pulls me up, I'm filled with excitement thinking about what could be at the other end.

It pulls me across the city and over the countryside.

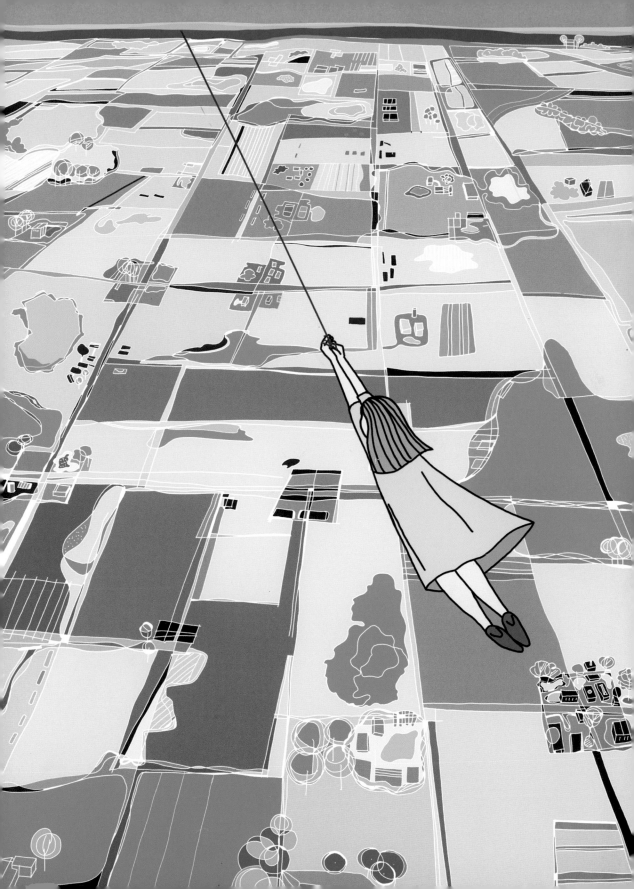

I don't know where
it will take me.

And then, it pulls me down.

It pulls me down to . . .

. . . You.

You need someone to take care of you.

You need someone to hug you, play with you and keep you warm —

someone to love you.

I will do that.

I'm your mother.

My thread becomes our thread. It keeps us together.

Our thread connects us as
you learn to play and
master new skills,

and as you discover the world around us.

Our thread is there as you make friends.

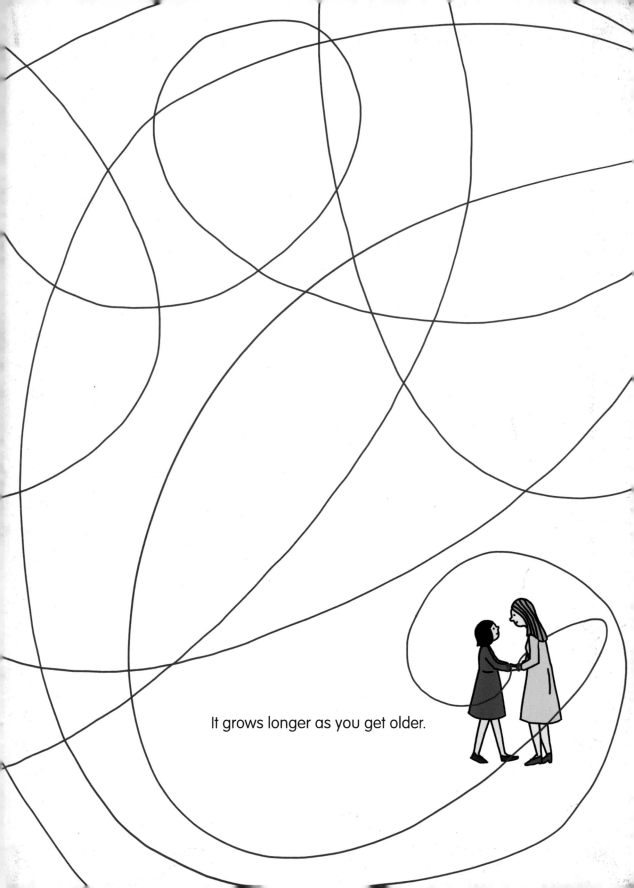

It grows longer as you get older.

One day you will be big enough to go out on your own.

The love we have for each other will
always stay in our hearts, even as you find your own way . . .

. . . and reach for your own thread.